HKJ

THE LITTLE BUTTERFLY THAT COULD

Where are the flowers?

ROSS BURACH

Scholastic Press New York

Oh, life was so much simpler as a caterpillar.

← me!

I easily built a chrysalis,

chrysalis
(I'm inside.)

patiently waited to become a butterfly,

Tada!

then began my journey with friends to find flowers.

But then . . .

. . . things got cloudy.

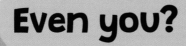

You are the **BIGGEST** creature in the ocean.

But the ocean is **BIGGER!** Sometimes I get butterflies in my stomach, too.

This is **WAY** more spacious than my chrysalis.

Hmm . . . Anything to eat other than krill? No? I'll just order in.

Hello . . . A bouquet of flowers, please. Extra nectar. The occasion? I'm hungry. My address? A whale.

– Click –

Hello? HELLOOO???

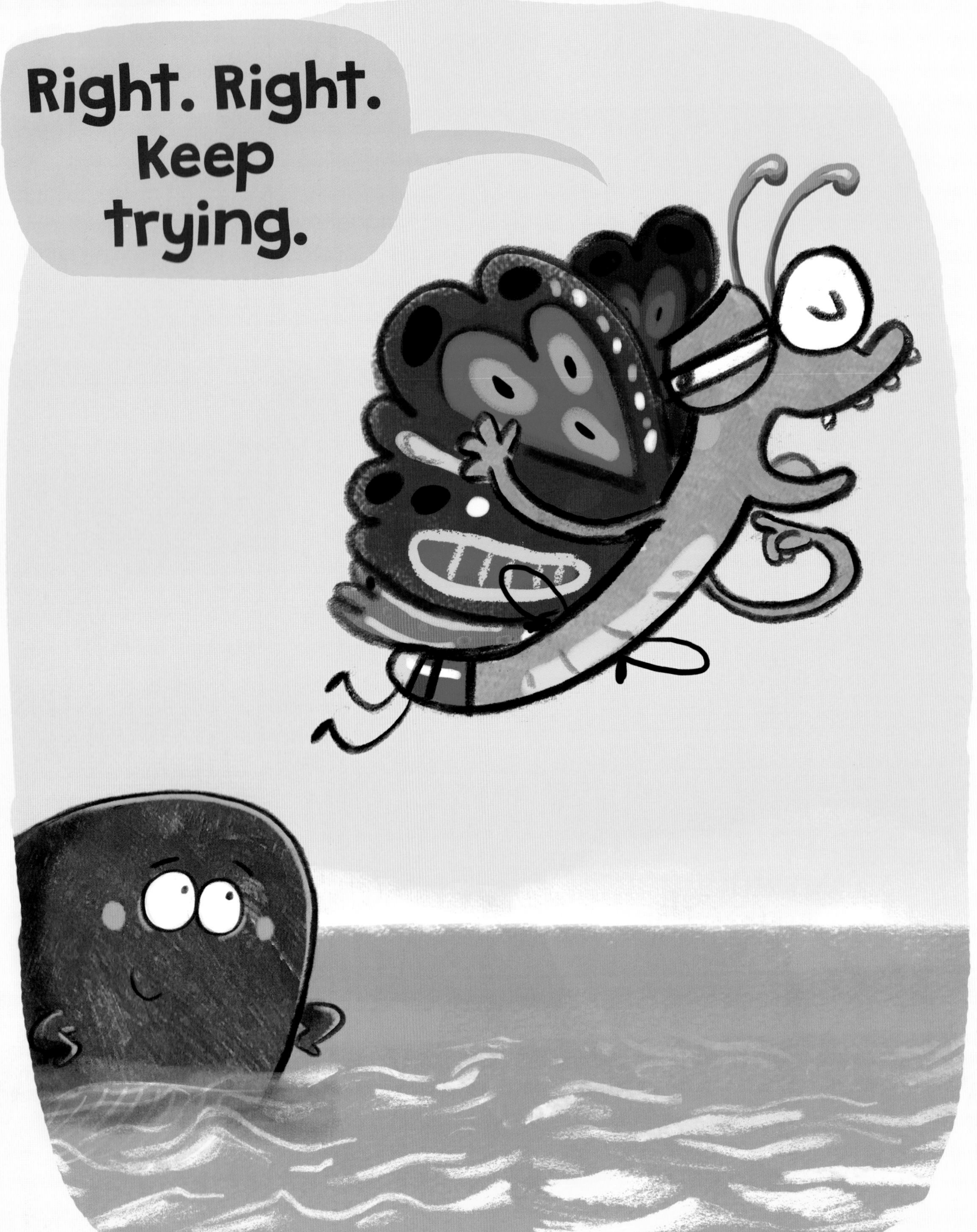
Right. Right. Keep trying.

200 miles. No problem.

Getting closer.

I can smell the flowers!

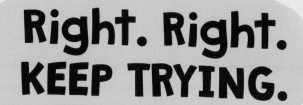

SPLAT!
Right back where I started.
I'll never get there.

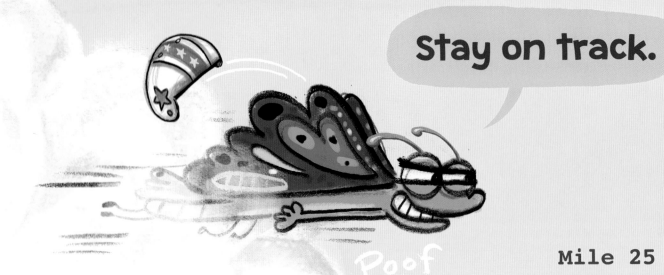

Keep trying.

Mile 125

Keep flying.

Mile 150

Keep trying.

200 miles later . . .

To Lara — for helping me find my way in picture books

Ross Burach's art was created with pencil, crayon, acrylic paint, and digital coloring. · The text type was set in Grandstander Classic Bold. · The display type was set in Grandstander Classic Bold. The book was printed on 157gsm Golden Sun matt paper and bound at RR Donnelly Asia. · Production was overseen by Catherine Weening. · Manufacturing was supervised by Shannon Rice. The book was art directed and designed by Marijka Kostiw, and edited by Tracy Mack.